CARTER HIGH
SENIOR YEAR

TIME TO
Move On

By Eleanor Robins

SADDLEBACK
EDUCATIONAL PUBLISHING

CARTER HIGH
SENIOR YEAR

SADDLEBACK
EDUCATIONAL PUBLISHING
www.sdlback.com

ISBN-13: 978-1-61651-329-0
ISBN-10: 1-61651-329-2
eBook: 978-1-60291-977-8

Printed in Guangzhou, China
0910/09-42-10

15 14 13 12 11   1 2 3 4 5

Chapter 1

Bel walked to school. It was the first school day after spring break.

Bel's real name was Belinda. But her friends called her Bel.

Paz walked with her. Paz was her best friend.

"I can hardly believe it, Bel. Our senior year will be over in less than two months. And we will be out of high school," Paz said.

"I know, Paz. It's hard to believe," Bel said.

"I hope this will be a great two months for us," Paz said.

"I hope it will be too," Bel said.

Bel was sure it would be a great time for her. She was dating Al.

Al was her boyfriend. His real name was Alberto. He and Bel dated for a year.

Paz said, "I am so glad you are back, Bel."

"So am I. And I am in a hurry to get to school. I can hardly wait to see Al," Bel said.

Bel and her mom had been out of town. Bel's aunt was sick. So Bel and her mom went to stay with her aunt. They also took care of her cousins.

Bel hadn't seen Al in over a week.

She missed Al, and she could hardly wait to talk to him. But most of all, she just wanted to see him.

Paz said, "I wanted to call you last night. I needed to talk to you about something. But I knew you would want to talk to Al, not me."

"I did want to talk to Al. But Al didn't call," Bel said.

Paz looked very surprised.

Paz asked, "He didn't call? Maybe he didn't know you would be home last night."

"But he did know. School starts back this morning. So he knew I would be home last night. I told him that before I left," Bel said.

Bel had been sure Al would call. She had wanted to call him. But she didn't think she should do that.

Bel asked, "How is Al? Do you know? I didn't hear from him at all. Not even one time. And he said he would call me at my aunt's house."

Paz looked even more surprised.

Then Paz said, "I haven't seen Al. He must be very busy. That must be why he didn't call."

The girls got to the school. Some students were standing outside the school.

Bel looked for Al. But she didn't see him.

Paz waved at someone.

Then Paz said, "I see Al, Bel."

"Where?" Bel asked.

Paz said. "He is over there. I waved at him. But he didn't see me."

Bel looked where Paz said Al was standing. Then she saw Al. But he wasn't looking their way.

Bel said, "I must go over there, Paz. It seems like a long time since I talked to Al. And I must talk to him before school starts."

Paz said, "OK. I will go on to class. I will see you after our first class."

"OK," Bel said.

Then Bel hurried over to Al.

Bel thought Al saw her. But he turned away. So he probably didn't see her. He started to go in the school.

Bel called to him. She said, "Al. Wait."

But Al didn't wait. So he must not have heard her.

Bel called to him again. She said, "Wait, Al."

Al stopped. And he turned around. But he didn't look happy to see Bel. That surprised her.

Bel said, "Al, I am so glad to see you. I have missed you so much."

But Al didn't say he had missed Bel.

"I thought you were going to call last night," Bel said.

But Al didn't say anything. And that wasn't like Al.

Al seemed upset.

"Is something wrong, Al?" Bel asked.

But Bel had a bad feeling. Now she

wasn't sure she wanted to know.

Al still didn't say anything. And he didn't look at Bel.

"Why didn't you call me last night?" Bel asked.

At first Al didn't answer.

But then he said, "I like you, Bel. I like you a lot. You are a very nice girl. But—."

He didn't say any more.

But he didn't need to say more. Bel knew what he wanted to say. He had found a new girl.

Bel said, "I know, Al. You have found a new girl. A girl you like better than me."

Al seemed surprised.

"You are right, Bel. But how do you know? Who told you?" Al asked.

Bel said, "No one, Al. But I know you wouldn't act this way unless you had found a new girl."

"I am sorry, Bel," Al said.

And Al did seem as if he was sorry.

"I am sorry too, Al. But it is OK. You must do what makes you happy," Bel said.

Bel didn't want to say that. But she made herself say it. And then she made herself say something else.

"Why didn't you call me, Al? Why didn't you tell me last night?" Bel asked.

"I know I should have, Bel. But I didn't know how to tell you. So I didn't call you," Al said.

"But you should have called, Al," Bel said.

Then Bel went in the school without Al.

Al had broken up with her.

The rest of her senior year wouldn't be so great after all.

Chapter 2

Bel went to class. But she couldn't keep her mind on the class. All she could think about was Al. She was glad he wasn't in any of her classes.

Bel wanted to talk to Paz. But her teacher didn't let her class out on time. So Bel wouldn't have time to tell Paz about Al.

Bel hurried out of her class. Paz was waiting for her in the hall.

Paz asked, "What is wrong, Bel? You don't look so good."

Bel said, "I don't have time to tell you now. But I need to talk to you, Paz."

Bel didn't think she would see Paz again until after school. They didn't have the same classes. And they didn't have lunch at the same time.

Bel said, "We might have to wait until after school to talk. And I don't think I can wait until then."

But Bel knew she would have to wait that long.

"It can't be that bad," Paz said.

Bel said, "But it is, Paz. It is. I wish I could tell you how bad it is now. But we have to get to our classes."

So Bel couldn't tell Paz.

Bel hurried to class. She was almost late. She couldn't keep her mind on the class. All she could think about was Al.

Bel had lunch next. But she didn't want to go to lunch. Al had lunch at the same time. And she didn't want to see him.

Bel walked slowly to the lunchroom.

She saw Marge. Marge had been in some of her classes last year. And she had been in the senior play with Bel.

Bel hoped Marge didn't see her. But Marge did see Bel.

Marge said, "Wait, Bel. I will walk with you."

Bel stopped. But she didn't want to wait for Marge. She knew Marge would ask her about Al.

Marge hurried up to Bel.

She said, "You don't look very well, Bel. What is wrong with you?"

"Nothing is wrong with me, Marge. I am fine," Bel said.

But that wasn't true.

Marge acted as if she didn't believe Bel.

Marge said, "I wish we had lunch at the same time. Then we could talk."

Bel was glad Marge didn't have lunch

with her. Bel didn't like to eat with Marge. Marge had eaten lunch with her and Paz last year. But Marge liked to talk about people. And sometimes what she said wasn't true.

Marge said, "Too bad I don't have lunch next. I have to get to class. I will see you later."

Marge hurried off. Bel was glad to be alone.

Bel got to the lunchroom.

She saw Juan.

Juan had dated Paz for most of the school year. Paz liked him, but not as much as he liked her.

Juan walked over to Bel.

Bel hoped Juan would talk to someone else and not to her. But she didn't want to be rude to Juan.

Juan said, "Hi, Bel. Was your spring break nice?"

"Yes," Bel said.

But that wasn't really true. She had wanted to be with Al, not with her sick aunt.

Juan said, "I would like to talk to you about something, Bel. But I see Al. And I know you are in a hurry to be with him."

Most days Bel had eaten lunch with Al. But she wouldn't eat with him anymore.

Juan would soon know about Bel and Al. She knew she should tell Juan. But she didn't want to talk about it.

Bel said, "I must get my tray, Juan. I will talk to you later."

"OK, Bel. I will talk to you later," Juan said.

Juan got his tray. He went to eat with some of his friends.

Bel got her tray. Then she saw Al. He looked over at her.

Bel decided she would act as if nothing was wrong between them. She would make herself speak to him.

But Al turned away. He didn't want to speak to her.

Bel quickly got her tray. She went to a table and sat down. No one came to eat with her. Bel she was glad. She just wanted to be by herself.

Chapter 3

The rest of the school day went very slowly for Bel. All she could think about was Al. And she couldn't keep her mind on her classes.

Bel was glad when the end of school bell rang. She thought the school day would never end.

She quickly picked up her books and hurried out in the hall. Bel wanted to leave school as soon as she could.

Paz came up to her. Paz seemed worried.

Paz said, "You still don't look so good, Bel. What is wrong?"

"I will meet you outside, Paz. And I will tell you then," Bel said.

"I will be only a few minutes, Bel. I just have to go to my locker. Wait for me. I will walk outside with you," Paz said.

But Bel didn't wait. She hurried out of the school. Then she slowly walked home. Bel knew Paz would catch up with her.

A few minutes later, Paz ran up to her.

Paz said, "Tell me now, Bel. What is wrong?"

"Al has found a new girl," Bel said.

Paz seemed surprised. But not as surprised as Bel thought she would be.

"Are you sure it's true?" Paz asked.

"Yes. It is true," Bel said.

Paz asked, "Who told you that? Did Marge tell you? You can't always believe what she says. You know she just likes to talk about people. And you know she gets her facts wrong sometimes."

"Marge didn't tell me. Al told me," Bel said.

At first Paz didn't say anything.

But then she asked, "Are you sure that is what Al said?"

"Yes," Bel said.

"I am sorry, Bel. I thought that must be why you were upset. I thought it had something to do with Al," Paz said.

"So that is why Al didn't call me last night. He didn't want to call me," Bel said.

At first Paz didn't say anything.

But then Paz said, "Al is a nice boy, Bel. He can't help it that he likes another girl now."

Bel said, "I know, Paz. But it doesn't hurt any less to know that."

"It will take some time, Bel. But you will find someone new too," Paz said.

Bel hoped that was true. She had dated other boys before she dated Al. But Al was the only boy she had ever really liked. Bel didn't think she would ever like any other boy as much as she liked Al.

Chapter 4

It was the next morning. Bel walked to school with Paz.

Paz asked, "Do you want to talk about Al?"

"No," Bel said.

Bel didn't want to talk about Al ever again. She wished she could forget all about him.

But Bel knew she should talk to Paz about something. So Paz wouldn't worry about her.

But what could they talk about?

Then Bel thought of something.

She said, "Yesterday you said you

needed to talk to me about something. What was it?"

"It is OK now, Bel. We don't need to talk about it," Paz said.

But Paz seemed upset. And Bel didn't think it was OK.

Bel had told Paz about Al. And Paz didn't seem as surprised as Bel thought she would be.

Did Paz know about Al before Bel told her? Was that what she needed to talk to Bel about? Bel didn't think it was. But Bel had to know.

Bel stopped walking. Paz stopped too. Then Bel looked at Paz.

Bel said, "I must ask you, Paz. Did you know about Al and his new girl?"

Paz seemed very surprised.

She said, "No, Bel, I didn't know. I wouldn't have wanted to tell you, but we are best friends. I would have told you if

I knew."

Bel said, "That is what I thought, Paz. But I had to ask. What did you want to talk to me about?"

"I don't want to tell you now," Paz said.

"Why?" Bel asked.

At first Paz didn't answer.

But then she said, "It might upset you because of what Al said to you."

"Don't worry about that. Just tell me what is wrong," Bel said.

"It is about Juan. I thought a lot about him over spring break. I like Juan. He is a nice boy," Paz said.

That was the same thing Al had said about Bel, right before she found out about his new girl.

Paz said, "I don't think I should date Juan anymore. I like him as a friend, but not as a boyfriend. I think I should tell Juan that."

Bel hoped that was the right thing for Paz to do.

Bel asked, "Are you sure you want to do that, Paz?"

"Yes. I am sure," Paz said.

"Is it because of Cruz?" Bel asked.

Paz had wanted to date Cruz for a long time. He had asked her to the spring dance last year. But Paz already had a date with Juan. And Cruz hadn't called Paz again.

Paz said, "Yes. I saw Cruz at the store over spring break. He said he might call me about a date. Maybe he might ask me for a date this weekend."

"But he might not, Paz," Bel said.

Bel knew Cruz liked a lot of girls. And Bel didn't think Cruz would be true to Paz.

Paz said, "I know. But I should still tell Juan. It isn't fair for me to date

Juan. He should know how I feel. Then maybe he will find someone else."

"When are you going to tell him?" Bel asked.

Paz said, "I will tell him this morning before school starts. I don't want to tell him then, but there isn't a good time to tell him."

Bel knew Paz was right about that.

The girls got to school. They saw Juan.

Paz said, "I shouldn't wait to do it. I am going to tell Juan now."

"Then I will see you later, Paz," Bel said.

Paz went to talk to Juan.

Bel went inside the school. Then she went to her class.

It was a long morning for Bel. She still thought about Al, not about her classwork.

Bel was glad when lunch time came.

She went to lunch. She saw Juan

outside the lunchroom door. He seemed to be waiting for someone.

Juan smiled at Bel.

He said, "Hi, Bel."

"Hi, Juan," Bel said.

Then Bel saw Al. Al saw her too. But he quickly looked away.

They weren't going to date each other anymore. But why didn't he speak to her?

Bel hurried in the lunchroom. Juan went in too.

Bel quickly got a tray. Then she went to a table and sat down.

She hoped no one came to sit with her. Bel just wanted to be left alone.

But Juan came over to her table.

Juan asked, "Are you waiting for someone, Bel?"

"No," Bel said.

Juan said, "I would like to eat with you. Is it OK for me to do that?"

"Yes," Bel said.

But it wasn't OK. She wanted to be by herself. But Bel didn't want to be rude to Juan.

Juan said, "I heard about you and Al, Bel. I was sorry to hear it."

Bel didn't say anything. What was there to say?

Juan said, "I know how you must feel, Bel. This morning Paz told me the same thing. She doesn't want to date me anymore."

"I know, Juan. Paz told me she was going to tell you how she felt. And I am sorry. I know how much you like Paz," Bel said.

"Don't worry, Bel. It's fine. Paz gave me a chance. But it wasn't to be. I will find someone else. And so will you," Juan said.

But that didn't make Bel feel any better.

Chapter 5

It was Friday. Bel was on her way to her last class. She was glad it was Friday. It had been a long week for her.

Bel saw Al. He looked her way. Bel knew Al saw her. But then he looked away.

Bel had seen Al many times. She knew he had seen her each time. But he didn't speak to her.

Marge called to Bel.

She said, "Wait, Bel. I will walk with you."

Bel waited for Marge. But she didn't want to walk with Marge.

Marge hurried up to Bel. The two girls walked down the hall.

Marge said, "Al didn't speak to you. But I know he saw you. I heard he broke up with you because he has a new girlfriend. You didn't break up with him. So why didn't he speak to you?"

"I don't know," Bel said.

Bel wished she knew. Al wasn't dating her anymore. But he could still speak to her.

So why didn't he speak to her? He broke up with her. It wasn't as if she broke up with him.

Marge asked, "Am I right, Bel? Al did break up with you, didn't he?"

Bel wanted to say she broke up with Al. Then Marge wouldn't feel sorry for her. But she couldn't lie. It wouldn't be fair to Al.

"Yes. Al broke up with me," Bel said.

"That is what I thought. It's too bad. I heard his girlfriend goes to Walker High. Do you think he has dated her for a long time? Maybe you just didn't know it." Marge said.

Bel didn't think it was true. But why did Marge have to say it?

But maybe it was true. Maybe that was why Al didn't want to speak to her. Maybe he thought she knew.

Bel got to her class. She was glad. Bel didn't want to talk to Marge anymore.

"This is my class, Marge," Bel said.

"OK. See you later," Marge said.

Marge hurried off. Then Bel went in her classroom.

Bel was upset. She couldn't keep her mind on her classwork. All she could think about Al and what Marge had said about him.

Bel was still upset when the end of school bell rang.

Bel quickly left the class. She hurried to her locker. She got the books she needed.

She saw Paz. The two girls went outside.

Paz said, "You don't look so good, Bel. What is wrong?"

"It is something Marge wanted to know about Al and his new girl," Bel said.

"What?" Paz asked.

"Did I think Al has been dating her for a long time? That maybe I just didn't know it," Bel said.

"I don't believe that, Bel. Al isn't that kind of boy," Paz said.

And Bel hadn't thought he was either. But now she wasn't so sure.

"Then why doesn't Al speak to me?" Bel asked.

"I don't know. Maybe he doesn't see you," Paz said.

But Bel knew Paz didn't believe that.

Sometimes Marge was wrong about things. But maybe Marge was right this time. Maybe Al had dated the girl for a long time. And Bel just didn't know it.

Chapter 6

Bel went out of town for the weekend. She had to go see her aunt. So she didn't talk to Paz again until Monday. The girls were on their way to school.

Paz seemed very happy.

She said, "I can hardly wait to tell you."

"What?" Bel asked.

Paz said, "Cruz called me after I got home on Friday. He asked me for a date. We went to a movie on Saturday night."

"I am happy for you, Paz," Bel said.

Paz wanted to date Cruz. So Bel was glad Paz had a date with him. But Cruz should have asked Paz sooner in the week.

Bel hoped it would work out for Paz and Cruz. But Bel didn't think it would. Cruz never dated any girl for very long.

Paz said, "I had a great time. And I asked him about Al's new girlfriend."

That surprised Bel.

"Why did you ask Cruz that?" Bel asked.

"Because you are my best friend, and you wanted to know," Paz said.

"What did Cruz say?" Bel asked.

"Al met his new girl when you were out of town. So he didn't know her before. He did date her while you were out of town. But he was true to you until then," Paz said.

That made Bel feel a little better, but not much better.

Bel believed what Cruz said was true. Cruz thought it was OK to date a lot of girls. So she didn't think he would lie for Al.

"Thank you for finding out for me, Paz," Bel said.

"That is what best friends are for," Paz said.

"Did you ask Cruz why Al won't speak to me?" Bel asked.

Paz said, "No. I didn't think you would want me to ask him that."

"And you were right, Paz," Bel said.

But Bel still wished she knew anyway.

Bel and Paz got to school. Bel didn't see Al then. But she did see him on her way to lunch. Al saw her too. But he didn't speak to her. That upset Bel very much.

Juan walked up to Bel.

Juan asked, "What is wrong, Bel?"

Bel told him.

Then she said, "And I haven't done anything to Al. So I don't know why Al won't speak to me."

Juan said, "I do, Bel. He feels bad because he broke up with you. And he doesn't know what to say to you. So he doesn't say anything."

"Thank you for telling me, Juan," Bel said.

It was hard for her to see Al. And it was harder still when he wouldn't speak to her. But now she knew it was hard for Al to see her too.

Bel didn't really want to talk to Al. But she and Al must talk, soon.

Chapter 7

Bel and Juan got to the lunchroom. Bel saw Al again. He stood outside the door.

Al saw Bel. But then he looked away.

Al didn't like Bel anymore. And he couldn't help it that he liked someone new. But he mustn't feel bad about that.

Bel didn't want to talk to Al. But she knew she must. Then maybe she would start to feel better.

Bel said, "Juan, I must talk to Al. I will talk to you later."

"OK, Bel. I hope all works out well for you," Juan said.

Bel walked over to Al.

Al seemed surprised.

Bel said, "We must talk, Al."

Al was upset.

Al said, "I don't have time to talk. I have to eat lunch."

He started to go in the lunchroom.

But they did have time to talk for a few minutes.

Bel said, "Wait, Al. We must talk."

Al stopped.

He said, "We have nothing to talk about, Bel. I am sorry. But it is over for us."

Bel said, "I know it is, Al. But we go to the same school. And we will still see each other. So we should be nice to each other."

Al didn't say anything.

"You aren't nice to me, Al. You look away when you see me. And you don't talk to me," Bel said.

"I am sorry, Bel. But I have told you. It is over for us. And there is nothing to say," Al said.

"You can look at me. And you can say hi. You don't have to say more," Bel said.

Al didn't say anything.

Bel said, "We don't date anymore. And I know we won't date anymore. But I hope we can still be friends, Al."

Bel didn't really want to be Al's friend. She wanted to be his girlfriend. But she knew it was too late for that.

They would still see each other a lot. And they would have to be friends, or it would be very hard for them to see each other.

Al said, "I don't know, Bel."

"We are the same people, Al. We just aren't dating anymore. But we should be friends," Bel said.

"Are you sure you want to be just a

friend and nothing else?" Al asked.

"Yes, Al," Bel said.

There was nothing else for her to be.

Al asked, "You really mean that, Bel? You aren't mad at me? You do just want to be friends?"

Bel said, "I am not mad at you, Al. You cannot help who you like."

Just as she couldn't help who she liked. But why did she have to like Al?

Al had moved on. So why couldn't she?

Al said, "Then friends we will be, Bel."

Al smiled at Bel. And she smiled at him. But it wasn't easy for Bel to smile back at him.

Bel knew it would be OK between them. But it would never be the same as before.

"You are very nice, Bel. I wish it had worked out for us," Al said.

Bel wished it had too. But it never would now.

Al said, "I need to eat, Bel. And so do you. I'm glad we talked."

"So am I," Bel said.

Bel felt better. She was glad she had talked to Al.

Chapter 8

Bel and Al went in the lunchroom. Bel and Al got their trays.

Bel went to a table, and she sat down. Al went to sit with a friend.

No one came to sit with Bel, and she was glad. Bel did feel better about Al. But she still wanted to eat by herself. She didn't want to talk to anyone.

Bel sat by herself for a few minutes. Then Juan walked over to her table.

Juan said, "I saw you smile at Al. I hope all is well with you and Al now. And I need to ask, Bel, are you two back together now?"

"No. Al has moved on. I need to move on too. But it won't be easy," Bel said.

Juan said, "Yes, it won't be easy. And I should move on too. Paz cannot help the way she feels."

"No, she can't," Bel said.

"I would like to eat lunch with you, Bel. Is that OK?" Juan asked.

"Yes," Bel said.

Bel didn't want to say yes, but she didn't want to be rude to Juan.

Juan sat down at the table.

He said, "We cannot date the person we want to date. But we should move on, Bel. It is right for us to do that."

"I know," Bel said.

But there was no one Bel wanted to date.

Bel and Juan ate for a few minutes. They didn't talk to each other.

Then Juan said, "I am going to a

movie on Friday night. Would you like to go with me, Bel?"

At first Bel didn't answer.

Then Juan said, "I know I am not Al. And I know you are not Paz. But we should go out on dates. And why not go out with each other?"

Bel didn't want to go out with Juan. She didn't want to go out with another boy. She never wanted to date again. But she was sure she wouldn't always feel that way.

But Juan knew she didn't have a date. And she didn't want to be rude to him.

So Bel said, "OK, Juan. I will go to the movie with you."

It was time for Bel to move on. She should try to find someone new. Bel didn't think her new boyfriend would be Juan. But she wouldn't know unless she went out with him.

The rest of the school year wouldn't be as much fun without Al. And her senior year wouldn't be as she thought it would be with Al. But she could still try to have a good time.